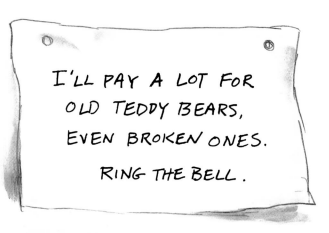

Illustrations © 1993 Gabrielle Vincent
Text © 1993 Christophe Gallaz
Translation © 1993 Creative Education, Inc.
Cover Design by Rita Marshall
The first edition of this book was published
in French by Editions Duculot.
Published in 1993 by Creative Editions
123 South Broad Street, Mankato, Minnesota 56001 USA
Creative Editions is an imprint of Creative Education, Inc.

The publication of this book
is a joint venture between Creative Education, Inc.
and American Education Publishing.
ISBN 1-56846-085-6
Printed in Belgium.

# THREADBEAR

ILLUSTRATIONS BY
GABRIELLE VINCENT

WRITTEN BY
CHRISTOPHE GALLAZ

CREATIVE EDITIONS

When the old man found me lying in the
street, I was lost and confused. I couldn't
remember how long I'd been there or where
I came from. I didn't even know who I was.

Fortunately the old man was kind enough
to bring me to his house. He set me down
on a table and saw that I needed a leg, so he
stitched one on. Then he asked me my
name, but I couldn't answer because I had
forgotten it.

  "We'll call you Threadbear," he said.

Titi

Rory

I soon noticed that there were lots of other
bears in the old man's house. Some were
bigger than me and others were smaller.
Some were lighter and some were darker.
But one thing we had in common was that
we were all very quiet.

George

Howie

Armstrong

We sat together for hours without speaking
a word or even looking at one another. We
were all trying to remember our pasts.

John John

Twisty

Every so often a quiet and lonely bear voice
would rise above the silence, and the rest of
us would turn to listen. Slowly, more of us
began to talk. We learned that the old man
had given each of us a name. We even
realized that some of us were from the same
towns, although we had never been friends.

Jackie

Andy

One of the very tattered teddy bears sat alone and vaguely remembered living through many changing seasons. This made him think that he must be very old. Maybe that was why he had been abandoned.

Elmer

Other more playful bears felt sure that they were very young.

Jerry

Jeannie

Sandy

Fifi

Grumps

At night we climbed into our beds and
talked until we grew sleepy. We knew there
were many more things we needed to
remember. We hoped that our dreams
might bring us the answers.

Harvey

Ned

Roy

One night a bear named Charlie decided to be a clown. He sat on a chair and made silly faces. He thought he was *really* funny when he hung a pacifier around his neck— but no one laughed.

Instead we each sat frozen with our memories of a baby sitting in a playpen or lying in a crib, a baby who had loved us a long time ago.

The weeks passed. I began to speak with the old man at night when I felt lonely. The picture of the child I had known, a little boy, came back to me. I could see his rosy-pink cheeks and curly blond hair. I remembered that he had hugged me, but sometimes he had also hit me.

I tried to ignore these memories, but I
couldn't. I wasn't sure why he acted like
that; I guessed I had done something wrong.
All I knew for certain is that he hurt me.

I felt better when the old man let me
sleep beside him. He laid my head on a
downy pillow and I forgot my sadness.

Just about every day the old man brought home more teddy bears, rescuing them from the gutters and garbage cans. Like us, they came from cities near and far. They, too, could remember children who had hugged and hit them, and they quickly became our friends.

While the old man patched up the injured teddy bears and cheered up the sad ones, the rest of us continued to talk. And as we laughed and cried, our memories joined together to fill the house like a song.

In this way we slowly came back to life. But sometimes our playfulness made the old man tired. Then he would gently slide into his armchair and quietly drop off to sleep. While he rested we watched over him, just as he always watched over us.

Like anxious children, however, we would ask
him to tell us stories the moment he awoke.
Once he told us about his own childhood:
   "I used to have teddy bears," he said.
"Like you, they were all different sizes and
colors." The old man paused for a moment,
looking down at the floor.

"I, too, hugged them—and hit them. I hurt my friends and they cried, but I couldn't see their tears. For years I didn't understand what had happened. I finally realized that I had hit the teddy bears not because of anything *they'd* done wrong, but because *I* was sick or angry or just in a bad mood.

"I had hurt them because I was unhappy."

Lisa

Felix

Pete

Lulu

Brownie

Sitting in silence, we waited for him to
continue.

But he simply shook his head and sighed,
"I'm sorry."

Scooby-doo

Fuzzy

Munchkin

us

Tuffie

Wuzzy

Theodore

Jupiter

Minnie

The old man's words stayed on our minds for a long time.

For days his house was quiet. Once again we sat without speaking a word or even looking at one another.

Murphy

Big Guy

Gradually, we began talking and
playing again. We began to look forward
to the future.

The old man went on doing his work. Every day he roamed the streets, finding more abandoned bears.

He gave these bears new legs or arms if they needed them. He even gave one bear a new head with blue eyes. After he fixed the teddy bears, he gave them names and introduced them to the rest of us.

Peter

Big bears and small ones, yellow ones and
brown ones—our differences didn't matter
because we all shared a common past.

There were many of us now. We were all
repaired and happy.

Tubby

As we played together in our house,
we continued to discover the old man's
kindness.

Tiny

Sybil

Oscar

Pe

Whiskers

Bibi

Gabby

Bruno

He loved us and it showed. Not only did we
have new legs and patches, but we were even
gaining weight!

Adolphus

Alex

Albert

Patrick

Lucky

Monica

Pom-pom

Dodo

Dexter

Lulu

Moe

Ralphie

Arthur

Sometimes we dressed up in overalls or
aprons and pretended to be real people.
   Other times we pretended to be hurt so
we could practice taking care of each other.

Alfie

Willy

As we became healthier, we didn't need as
much of the old man's attention, so he took
more time to read and write.

One day, however, he had a big surprise for
us. He took us out of our house and into
the warm sunshine for a walk. It had been a
long time since we had felt the fresh air.

As he strolled along, the old man hugged us tight. A few people smiled at us as we walked by. Some even stopped to pet us and chat.

Wandering through the streets, the old man
spoke of the time we had spent together. He
also reminded us about what he had learned
from his childhood. "One day," the old man
told us gently, "you'll be going back out
into the world."

NOTHING FOR SALE.

Several days later, a stranger came knocking
at the door. "Old man, I'll give you all this
money for that bunch of bears," he said gruffly.
   "What? Sell them?" exclaimed the old
man. "Never!"
   We were relieved when the stranger
stormed away.

One afternoon, a little girl rang our
doorbell. The old man invited her in to
meet us, and her eyes grew bright and wide
as he told her our story. Then he gathered
my friends together one by one and softly
placed them in her arms.

I alone stayed with the old man—we still
had so much to say to each other.